BASKETBALL TOSS-UP

ALEX B. ALLEN

Basketball
Toss-Up

pictures by Kevin Royt

ALBERT WHITMAN & Company, Chicago

Library of Congress Cataloging in Publication Data

Allen, Alex B
  Basketball toss-up.

  SUMMARY: Jamie finds himself a reluctant participant
on his brother's basketball team in the big game with a
rival boys club.
  [1. Basketball—Stories]   I. Royt, Kevin, illus.
II. Title.
PZ7.A4217Bas   [Fic]   72–83680
ISBN 0–8075–0578–1

To Kathy Aycrigg and Cap

Contents

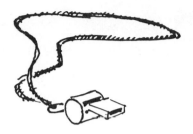

1 · Bad Luck

Jack hated to be late for basketball practice. But he couldn't help it. He'd had to help his twin, Jamie, find their dog. They'd looked and looked. Baron was still lost.

Now Jack ran into the Boys Club gym. "What a mess!" he thought. "Captain of the team, and I'm late for practice on the day before the big game."

Coach Watkins was watching the team play.

Roy was throwing a long pass to Stringer, who had streaked down the court to catch the pass.

Stringer was a great center, Jack thought, as he watched. He was good at driving in for fast lay-up shots.

Jack saw that the forwards, Fred and Andy, were slow on their feet. They weren't finding the opening for an easy shot. Something was wrong. They'd always been great.

"Guess they're tense because of the game with the Red Devils," thought Jack to himself. "We want to beat them. We never have. And if we play this way tomorrow, we never will."

Jack shook his head. It was bad.

The club coach blew his whistle. Action stopped on the court. Coach Watkins glanced at Jack.

He said, "Glad you're here, Jack. Maybe you'll be the spark we need."

"Sorry to be late, Coach. But I just had to help Jamie track Baron down. No luck." He sighed. "Dad will blow up when he hears that dog is lost again."

Coach Watkins looked at the boys.

"Stringer, get in and nab more of those rebounds!"

He looked at Fred. "Fred!" he boomed. "Are you feeling all right?"

"I'm a little rocky, I guess, Coach. But I'll be tip-top by tomorrow's game. Honest."

Jack walked over to Fred and patted his head. "A little rocky? I've been watching you. You're dead on your big feet, chum."

Fred grinned.

"Okay, guys, let's go," Coach Watkins called. "You too, Jack. All of you—watch that ball! Remember, the team that grabs the most rebounds is the team that wins."

The boys swung into action.

When the coach stopped the game again, he waved the players over to the bench.

"Wow," said Fred, "it sure feels good to sit down."

"You can say that again," panted Andy.

"Okay," grinned Fred. "Wow, it sure feels good to sit down."

The boys laughed with the coach.

"Okay, you guys," he said. "Who's going

to win tomorrow? The Blue Rangers—or the Red Devils?"

"How can you ask, Coach?" asked Jack. "Blue Rangers, hands down. Right, team?"

"Right!" they all shouted.

"I sure hope so," said the coach. "Your teamwork is a lot better than it was last year. And every single one of you has grown." He looked around. "Not just taller," he added. "Better."

"Go, team!" said Stringer.

"But *they're* better, too," said the coach. "Remember how that club took you to the cleaners last year?"

Jack remembered. Jamie was playing on the team back then. Jamie got the ball—and threw it to a Red Devil by mistake. That had lost the Blue Rangers the big game of the season.

When the boys had started to play ball again this season, Jamie had come out for the first practice. But he couldn't forget that

he'd made his team lose the big game. He didn't play again all season.

Jamie's name was still on the club roster of players. But Jack had given up trying to get Jamie back on the court.

Jack looked around at the team. They could really use Jamie tomorrow. But what was the use of thinking about it? Jamie wouldn't play. He was afraid he'd let the team down again.

The boys broke up.

Jack walked home, scuffing his sneakers on the sidewalk. Then he glanced up. Coming toward him at a run was Jamie.

"No sign of Baron yet," said Jamie. "I've looked everywhere."

Jack frowned. "Gee," he said, worried. "If that dog has chased one more car—and if he's been picked up one more time by the dog-catcher—he's really in trouble."

"So are we," added Jamie. "Dad said if Baron landed in the dog pound once more, he'd give him away. We've *got* to find him."

The boys looked around helplessly. "Baron, Baron!" They whistled the special whistle that always brought the big dog running, tail wagging.

But there was no Baron.

The boys walked home, still looking and calling and whistling.

2 · One More Chance

Jack and Jamie burst into the house shouting, "Mom, where are you?"

"In the kitchen, for a change," called Mrs. Miller. "Where else do people find mothers? Dancing by candlelight?"

"Has Baron come back yet? Have you seen him?" they asked. "We've looked all over."

She shook her head. "I haven't seen him, but the dog pound has. That's where he is. And Dad's over there now, bailing him out. The *last* time he did that he said it would be the last time. Now he says *this* is the last time.

There won't *be* another time. Getting Baron out of the pound has become a full-time job. And Dad already *has* a job."

"What'll we do?" asked Jamie.

"Just what Dad's been telling you all along. You'll have to train that collie. Not next week. Now."

"He *is* trained, Mom," said Jamie.

"He is? That's news," their mother said. Then she smiled at the twin. "Dad will give you and Baron one more chance."

"I've been training him for weeks, Mom," Jamie said. "He's really smart. You should see the things I've taught him."

"Anyone can see you haven't taught him to stay out of the street. He's always chasing cars. And you know how strict the city rules are now. He's picked up by the dog pound truck every time. And every time, your father has had to bail him out. And every time he has to bail him out, he gets mad. And every time he gets mad . . ."

"I know," said Jamie. "Please tell Dad it's never going to happen again."

"I'll *tell* him again. But you'll have to be the ones to *show* him. I'm all talked out."

"Honest, Mom, I'm going to spend every free second training him," said Jamie.

"And I'll help train him, too, when the game is over," said Jack.

"It would take a team of experts working around the clock to train that dog," said their mother. "But don't count on me. I'm still trying to train *you*."

"We can keep him fenced in the yard when we're not home. He'll be all right there. He can't jump the fence," said Jamie.

His mother shook her head and sighed. "Not yet," she said. "But the day will come when he can. And it will come soon. He's growing like a weed."

"Hey, Jamie," Jack called. "Come on—be a pal and practice shooting baskets with me while we're waiting for Dad to bring Baron back. I've got to practice as much as I can before the game."

The boys grabbed the ball out of the closet and ran to the driveway.

"Let's do our twenty foul shots apiece," said Jamie.

For months the boys had kept a chart of their scores. That made their practice fun.

"You win every time, Jamie," Jack complained as Jamie kept sinking one shot after another. "You always get at least fifteen out of twenty. And I'm still plugging along with twelve out of twenty, if I'm lucky. Guess you must have a better eye."

Jamie laughed and landed another basket. It was true. He did have a better eye. And he was fast.

Jack shook his head. He knew Jamie remembered that last game he'd played—that big important game with the Red Devils. It was near the end of that close game that Jamie had thrown the ball to a Devil. The guard had flipped in the winning basket. *The* important game was lost.

Everyone had teased Jamie. "Which way's up, Jamie?" "Whose team are you on, kid?" "Wrong-way Jamie!" "Where are your glasses?" Nobody really blamed him. They had just teased. But it had hurt Jamie. It had hurt a lot.

Now Jack wondered if throwing baskets in the driveway was what Jamie really wanted. Or did Jamie ever miss playing with the team? He never wanted to talk about it.

"Tell you what," said Jack. "Coach said half the game is getting rebounds. Miss a few so I can practice. Okay?"

"Miss a few? And mess up my record? Not a chance," said Jamie.

"Come on," said Jack. "This won't count on our chart."

At that moment the boys heard the car coming.

"I hope Dad has Baron with him," said

Jamie, running over to the car as it pulled into the driveway.

Baron was in the car, wagging his tail happily.

Their father was less cheerful.

"Baron may think he's a hero or something," he announced, "but he's not. One more trip to the pound and he won't be coming back here. We'll give him away. I mean it. I've said it before and I say it again. That was my last trip to bail him out. You train him or else. There must be a brain hiding somewhere in that head of his. Teach him something. Now."

"I have been training him, Dad," said Jamie. "He's really doing great. Just watch."

Mr. Miller folded his arms and watched.

"Heel, Baron," said Jamie. "See, Dad? He heels. Now watch. Sit! Sit! Baron, sit!" said Jamie.

Baron wagged his tail. "SIT, boy," said Jamie louder. And finally Baron sat down and yawned.

"Very good," said Mr. Miller. "Congratulations. Of course you know he sat down only because he was tired. And as for that dog being bright—it might interest you to know that the car he was chasing this time was the truck of the dogcatcher. He followed it all the way to the dog pound."

Mr. Miller went into the house and slammed the door.

Jamie turned to the dog. "Baron, you're going to have to learn—in a hurry."

"Honest, Jamie," said Jack, "right after to-morrow's game I'll really start working with you on Baron. I haven't done one thing to help you with him. So it's really partly my fault."

The twins returned to their game and played for a few minutes.

"I'm improving!" said Jack. "At least I'm ahead: six out of ten—and you have only five."

"You're not getting any better, I'm just getting worse," snorted Jamie. "I'm trying to keep my eye on Baron. He wants to chase the ball. He keeps getting up. My eye's more on him than on the basket, I guess."

"Make him lie down or something so we can practice some more rebounds."

"Baron! Lie down! Lie DOWN!"

Baron stretched out happily and closed his eyes.

Just then the twins' sister Jill rode her bike into the driveway.

"Hey, guess what!" she said. "Emily and

Nancy and I are going to be your cheerleaders at the game tomorrow. We're all going to dress alike. Blue skirts and white blouses. And we've made headbands that say 'Go Blue Rangers.' Isn't that exciting?"

"Oh, no," groaned Jack. "You'll get us laughed right off the floor. Nobody's got cheerleaders."

"Well, you do," said Jill.

"Well, we don't need any," said Jack.

"It was Emily's idea. She thinks you're cute."

"Cute!" Jack made a face. "Emily's crazy."

"Wait till you hear the cheer," said Jill. "It's wonderful. Besides, this is good practice for us. In a couple of years we can be real cheerleaders. As soon as we get in junior high."

"You'll never make junior high. You're all too dumb," said Jack.

"Who's dumb?" asked Jill. "Emily and Nancy are on the honor roll. You're not."

Jill watched them sinking baskets. "You

have to listen to the cheer. We worked all weekend on it."

Jack sighed. She was getting her whiny voice.

"Okay, let's hear it," said Jamie, throwing a basket.

"I can't do it unless you watch me. Watch," she said.

"How come we have to look?" asked Jamie, getting set for his next shot. "We can hear you without watching you, for Pete's sake."

"Silly, the best part is the action," she said. "Come on, watch!"

Sighing, the boys turned to watch.

"Ready?" asked Jill.

"Go, Blue Rangers, GO!
Win, Blue Rangers, WIN!
Go, Go, GO! . . ."

That was as far as Jill got with the new cheer. At that moment Baron jumped up and ran excitedly over to her. He jumped up on her, wagging his tail madly.

25

"Down, Baron," said Jill. "Honestly, that dog has no manners. Now I have to start all over again. Go, Blue Rangers, GO! . . ."

But Baron was jumping up on her again.

Jamie laughed. "Guess Baron's going to grow up to be a cheerleader, too," he said. "Come on, Baron, lie down! *Lie down!*" He sighed.

"Now, come on, watch," said Jill impatiently, starting to go into her cheer again.

"Hey, you know something? Cheerleaders get more exercise than the players," said Jack.

"I know," said Jill. Baron jumped up on her again. "And we're prettier, too," she said, running into the house.

3 · Jack's Promise

Dinner was over. The Millers were sitting around the table. It was time for dessert.

"Hey," said Jill. "I have to show everybody the cheer."

Jack groaned. "Mom, tell Jill she can't do this. She and Nancy and that stupid Emily want to be our cheering section. No club has cheerleaders. Everybody will make fun of us."

"Now, now Jack," said Mrs. Miller. "I think it's nice of the girls to be interested in the game."

"Emily isn't interested in basketball at all," said Jill. "She doesn't even like basketball. She likes Jack."

"Enough chatter, kids. Let's have some of Mom's blueberry pie," said their father.

"Not me, Mom," said Jack. "I've got to keep in shape for tomorrow's game."

"You mean I worked over a hot stove for nothing?" laughed Mrs. Miller.

"For nothing?" howled Jamie. "How about the rest of us?"

"Can I have Jack's piece?" asked Jill.

The telephone rang.

"I'll get it," said Jill, jumping up and running down the hall. "It's probably Emily or Nancy for me. About tomorrow."

They heard her voice: "Oh. Just a minute, Mr. Watkins. I'll call him."

Jack jumped up. "Wonder what Coach wants?" he said.

"Probably just wants to tell you that you can't have this pie of Mom's," laughed Mr. Miller. "Actually, we should make a pie like this for him. He's been such a nice guy, giving his time to the Boys Club."

Jill returned to the table as Jack answered the phone. They could all tell something was wrong.

"Oh, no, Coach. You've gotta be kidding! Fred and Andy both out? Any chance of either of them playing? Not at all? I don't know,

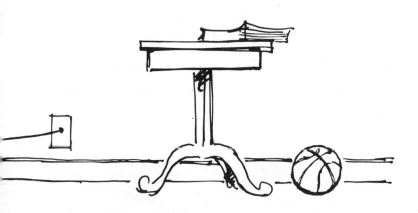

Coach, I don't know. The other subs are really too slow." There was a pause.

"Hey! Wait a second. I've got a super idea! My brother Jamie—you remember him. He's a terrific basketball player—you know that. He's a much better shot than I am. And the fastest thing in town. He'd be glad to help out, I know he would."

Jack listened a moment, then said, "Well, no, he hasn't been playing. But his name is still on the roster. He's been practicing a lot, shooting baskets, playing with me. I'll talk him into it. Oh, sure, Coach. Okay, see you tomorrow."

Jack ran into the dining room. Before he could say anything, Jamie said, "I heard you. What are you trying to do to me? I'm no basketball player. You know that."

"You're a better basketball player than all the rest of us put together. Jamie, you've just got to help out. Anyway, you'll just be warming the bench the whole time. You won't have to do anything at all—unless something happens."

"Unless something happens? What happened in the first place that you need ME to warm the bench?"

"Well, what's happened is that now Fred and Andy have the flu," explained Jack. "So both first-string forwards are goners. Talk about picking a bad time to be sick!"

"Yeah," said Jamie. "But you've already got subs to replace them."

"Sure we have, but both subs are going to be playing now, and we've got to have backups for them. Falk and Sonny are the subs. They can fill in for Fred and Andy. So—we need you to be a backup in case Falk or Sonny fouls out."

Jamie was shaking his head. "No way."

Jack added hastily, "They won't foul out, though. They're not the kind of guys who take chances. They'll play it safe. I'm sure they will."

Mr. Miller turned to Jamie. "Actually, you'd be a substitute for a substitute. A backup back-up. It's really a free front row ticket. Hey, sounds good! Can I sit on the bench, too? Best seat in the gym!"

"Do they have substitute bench warmers, too?" asked Mrs. Miller. "Because I could be one and get to see the game up close, too."

"Gee, Jack, I don't know," said Jamie. "I don't mind shooting a few with you in the driveway. You know, that's fun. But this is game stuff. I don't want to get tangled up in that sort of thing again. Ever. If I got called into the game, I'd—"

"Chances are you won't," said Jack.

"And if you did, Jamie, you'd do a great job," added Mr. Miller.

"I promised the coach you wouldn't let us down," said Jack. "I *promised*."

"I know," said Jamie. "Think I'm deaf?" He thought for a moment. "Well—I don't want to—but I guess I have to. I'd better not have to do anything. I'll be happy just to sit in that front row seat and watch you guys do all the work. And all the worrying. Well, yeah, I'll do it. What about a uniform?"

"I'll take care of that," Jack promised.

"Good," said Mr. Miller. "I'm glad you decided to help out, Jamie. It will be fun for Mom and me to have two of our kids involved in the big night—even if one of you is only a bench warmer."

"I hope I'll be only a bench warmer!" said Jamie.

"What about me?" asked Jill. "I'll be in it. I'll be cheering."

"That's right," said Mr. Miller. "One player, one bench warmer, and one cheerleader."

"And two watchers," said Mrs. Miller. "Dad and I wouldn't miss the game for anything."

"Wait till you hear the new cheer Emily and Nancy and I made up," said Jill. "It's a cheer against the Red Devils."

"How can you have a cheer against?" asked

her mother. "You cheer for something."

"Here's how it goes," said Jill, jumping up. "Get the Devils down! Get the Devils out!"

"Seems to me the Blue Rangers could use some of that pep tomorrow," said Mr. Miller.

"Excuse me, Mom," said Jack. "I'll have to get busy on the phone right now. We'll have to have an early morning practice here so we can all get in the swing of playing together."

"Good," said Jamie. "I'll need a rundown on the zone defense. And some practice on rebounding, too."

"More mouths to feed," said Mrs. Miller.

"Relax, Mom. We'll be too excited to eat," Jack said. "And too busy. But if you have any bananas lying around, or oranges . . ."

He counted on his fingers. "Let's see. Stringer, Roy, Falk, Sonny. Four of them. Plus me." He looked at his twin. "And Jamie."

Jamie started to hiccup. He always did that when he was nervous. And he was nervous now. Jack could have told that a mile away.

4 · Game Time

Jack knew that it had been a long Saturday for Jamie. And it wasn't even time for the game yet. He noticed his twin hadn't been able to eat breakfast or lunch. "Well, I'm excited too, I guess," thought Jack.

Now they were shooting some baskets in the driveway. And for the first time all day Jamie seemed to relax. He seemed to forget about the game.

Before they knew it, Mrs. Miller was calling to them. "I thought you wanted to get over to the club gym early," she called.

"What time is it?" asked Jack.

"Overtime," she said. "It's twenty past two."

"We were supposed to be there by now!" exclaimed Jack.

"I'll drive you over," Mrs. Miller said. "But we'll have to hurry."

The boys flung themselves into the car.

"Hey, how about Baron?" Mrs. Miller asked.

Jack noted with pride that Baron was still lying down where Jamie had told him to stay.

"I'll put him in the yard," said Jamie, leaping out of the car. "Here, Baron!" Baron rose.

"Coming when called," said Jamie. "Good boy!" Baron followed him into the yard.

"Hurry up!" called Jack.

Jamie latched the gate of the fence and raced over to the car.

Mrs. Miller pulled out of the driveway and drove down the street.

"We'll never make it!" complained Jack. "Hurry, Mom!"

"I can't hurry this stoplight. Red means

stop." As Mrs. Miller glanced into the rear-view mirror, she said, "I see we have someone following us."

Two heads swung around to see Baron happily running along the street. He was trying to catch up.

Jack groaned. "Oh, no! He can jump that fence."

"Smart dog," said Jamie.

"Well, there's only one thing to do for now," said Mrs. Miller. "Put Baron in the car with us and I'll get you to the gym in time and . . . and what will we do with Baron? Maybe he can join the Boys Club, until he learns something."

Baron leaped into the car happily and they drove on to the gym. Mrs. Miller sighed as the boys piled out of the car, leaving her with Baron. "You silly dog," she said, patting him. "You don't deserve us."

While the boys changed in the locker room, Mrs. Miller took Baron home and locked him in the house.

The boys were in the gym. Jamie gulped as it started to fill with people. It was a bigger crowd than any of them had expected.

Jack glanced over at his twin. Maybe he shouldn't have tried to talk Jamie into this. If anything happened this time, Jamie would never be able to get over it. But Jack wouldn't let himself think about that. He set his jaw. It just had to work out all right for Jamie this time.

The tense moment came: the beginning of the game.

Stringer, Jack, Roy, Falk, and Sonny took their places on the floor.

Stringer was ready for the jump. The whistle blew. The ball was tossed.

Stringer tipped the ball to Sonny. Sonny pivoted and shot a short bullet pass to Falk. Falk took a jump shot for the basket. The ball rolled around the rim, but did not drop in.

The Red Devils' center grabbed the rebound. He threw a long pass to his waiting forward. His forward caught the pass and quickly dribbled in toward the basket for a perfect lay-up shot.

The two points went up on the scoreboard.

Jack grabbed the ball at the end line. The Red Devils had sped down to defend their goal. Jack fired a short pass to Roy, who dribbled it over the center line, looking to see if Stringer was in a position for a jump shot.

Roy fired the ball to Stringer. The Red Devils had zoned him out. There was no opening to drive in for a lay-up. The seconds ticked off. Stringer had to get rid of the ball.

He shot a quick pass to Falk. A Red Devil

guard tore in and intercepted it. He quickly tossed a long pass to one of his teammates, a tall thin boy with red hair. The redhead lunged forward, plucked the ball out of the air, and tossed it into the basket.

The Red Devils now led: 4 to 0.

Back and forth the ball went. Seconds passed. Neither team could score. This made both teams nervous. They tightened up. The result: Sonny fouled by charging into a Red Devil. The free throw was sunk.

The score was 5 to 0.

"It's 5 to 0," said Jamie out loud, sitting on the bench. "It's going to be tough."

Within seconds after the ball was in play again, the Red Devil center fouled Jack when he tried to get the ball.

One free throw was awarded to Jack.

"Steady, boy," Jamie said under his breath as the ball was tossed to Jack for his free throw.

Jack's shot swished in.

The score was 5 to 1, with one minute to go before the end of the first quarter.

And in that minute the Red Devils sank one basket.

Then Stringer sank a lucky one.

When the whistle blew at the end of the first quarter, the Blue Rangers were really worried. And they had reason to be. The score: Red Devils—7, Blue Rangers—3.

5 · Tie Score

"We're losing the game," thought Jack desperately.

The boys were halfway through the second quarter, and the score was steadily inching up for the Red Devils.

"What's the matter with our guys?" wondered Jack. "They're dragging."

As Jack dribbled the ball over the center line, he said, "Steady, gang—let's go!"

He threw a two-handed pass to Falk, then ran to follow his own pass to provide a block for a set shot for Falk.

Falk arched a beautiful set shot through the basket.

That seemed to pull the team into action, and for a few minutes they really played their best. "Good," thought Jack. "We're moving now. About time!"

The score stood at 12 to 7. The Red Devils were still ahead, but the Blue Rangers were gaining.

The play teetered back and forth. Then the Red Devils went into a scoring surge. And the Blue Rangers were missing the very few shots they tried.

Now it was 18 to 7. "What's wrong?" Jack wondered.

Something had to be changed. But what? Someone had to be replaced—but who? Jack glanced at the coach.

The coach nodded to his sub center. Time-out was called.

Jack said quickly to the regulars around him: "A minute and a half more to go before half time. Let's try man-to-man defense and get that ball every chance we've got."

A minute of the game went by. The Red Devils spun in another basket.

On the scoreboard: 20 to 7.

Coach Watkins signaled Jamie. Jamie was to replace Falk. Jack looked at Jamie. He seemed in a daze. But in he went.

While Jamie still acted as if in a trance, and riveted to one spot, the Red Devil center charged into him. The referee blew his whistle and awarded Jamie one free throw.

Jamie went to the free throw line. The two teams took positions along the free throw lane. "Easy, Jamie," said Jack.

"Jamie looks scared," thought Jack, worrying. "I know he's thinking how he lost us our last game with the Red Devils." But Jamie automatically tossed in his free throw.

The score was now 20 to 8.

As the boys broke up, Jack pounded his twin on the shoulder. "Great going, Jamie! All that practice is paying off. You're coming through on automatic pilot!"

Before the Red Devils had a chance to move the ball beyond the center line, the half time buzzer went off.

Mr. and Mrs. Miller looked for Jill in the audience. Finally Mrs. Miller spotted her.

"At the last minute, Nancy must have been afraid to cheer. I see Jill dragging poor Emily out in front of everyone."

The two girls were nudging each other and giggling. Then they started their cheer.

"Jill hasn't a shy bone in her body," said Mrs. Miller. "She really puts everything she's got into it, doesn't she?"

"Mmmm," said Mr. Miller. "Including her muscles. She's all over the place. An acrobat at heart. And her voice—you can hear it over all this hubbub. Listen."

> "Get the Devils down!
> Get the Devils out!
> Race the Devils,
> Chase the Devils,
> WIPE—THEM—OUT!"

45

"All that shouting about Devils!" said Mrs. Miller. "It sounds like a late late horror show!"

"Rangers all right—
Devils all wrong!
Chase the Devils out of here,
Back where they belong!"

"Sounds like a TV commercial to me," said Mr. Miller, listening. "Maybe she could go into advertising instead of acrobatics."

Meantime, the coach was talking to the boys in the locker room. "Look guys, play as

a team. Guards—watch that left-handed forward. Close guard his left side. He never throws a pass with his right hand."

Roy and Jack nodded. "Right, Coach."

"Stringer, you're going to start out again. You were too tense. Relax, boy. You're better than your opposing center—he's just taking the game more in stride."

"I am a little tight," Stringer admitted. "I'll try to loosen up, Coach. I promise."

"Falk, one more foul and you'll be out of

the game. You're not thinking. You're careless. Don't try to plow through the other team."

"Coach is right," thought Jack. "Falk is being careless. It's not like him."

"Now all of you—relax. You're all tied up in knots. That's why you're missing so many baskets. You're letting them scare you. You're really better shots than they are. Usually you're better shots, that is. Come on! You can take this team! Go to it!"

Mr. and Mrs. Miller could see that Jill had talked Nancy into cheering. They could hear the sound of the three girls' shrill voices.

"Go, Rangers, GO!
Win, Rangers, WIN!
Go-go-go, Rangers, go and win!"

"So that's how that cheer ends," said Mrs. Miller. "I was betting on 'Let's begin!'"

"Speaking of beginning," said Mr. Miller, "they're about to. Half time's almost over." He watched the team come in. "And if they're going to score, they'd better start now."

After two minutes of the third quarter had gone by, another foul was called on Falk. He was out of the game.

There was nothing to do but put Jamie in. He was the only good substitute forward.

This time Jamie seemed in control of himself, thought Jack. That good throw must have given him confidence. Jack grinned.

Jamie broke up one Red Devil play, then another. Every time he had a shot, he made it. Everyone was amazed. Three baskets!. The rest of the team began to rally.

Jack thought proudly to himself, "Boy, Jamie is really with it! He's added six points to our score. And he's getting the team inspired!"

Jack found himself next to his twin for a few free seconds. "Terrific work, kid!" he grinned. "I'm playing better myself!"

The game moved into the last quarter. Quickly the Blue Rangers, inspired by Jamie's performance, pushed ahead and almost closed the gap in the score.

It was now 22 for the Red Devils, 18 for the Blue Rangers.

Four more points for a tie. Five for a win. Would there be enough time?

Jack took a deep breath.

Did the referee see Sonny's foul?

The whistle blew. That answered Jack's unspoken question. Now Sonny was out—out of the game on fouls.

Jack called a time-out.

There had to be a snap decision. He glanced at the coach. The coach nodded. There was only one solution. They had no good substitute forwards, so only one thing could be done. Jack would have to switch from guard to forward. The coach was already sending in a substitute guard.

Jack and Jamie were now the Blue Ranger forwards. They looked at each other and smiled.

Jack whispered, "It's like being back on the driveway, kid!"

Jack glanced at the scoreboard and at the clock. They showed 22 to 18 and two minutes to go.

"All right, guys," he said quickly. "We've got to make four points in two minutes to tie it up. Let's aim for six and take the game. Keep your cool."

Inspired, Jack nabbed the rebound from the Red Devils' free throw and fired a pass to Roy. Roy heaved it to Jamie. Jamie took a jump shot that angled beautifully through the basket.

The twins had never worked so well together. In less than a minute and a half they had tied the game, 22 to 22.

But the Red Devils were hanging onto their cool, too, as well as onto the ball. Seconds sped by. It was plain they were stalling, allowing time for just one shot. And they knew that the one shot had to be theirs. The winning shot!

The Blue Rangers were on man-to-man defense. Somehow they had to intercept the ball before time ran out.

The Boys Club gym was in an uproar.

Subs were no longer sitting on the squad bench. They were on their feet. The clock moved steadily on. Seven seconds . . . six . . . five . . .

And then the Red Devil forward fumbled the ball!

Jack shot in, grabbed it, and heaved one long pass to Jamie. Jamie raced to the left of the Red Devils' free throw lane and arched a shot.

The ball was in midair when the second hand of the clock hit zero. The ball rolled around the basket rim, and dropped out. No score.

The whistle blew.

It was still a tie: 22 to 22.

People on both sides of the gym were standing and cheering wildly.

The time signal for the beginning of the first overtime could barely be heard through the din.

But as play began, the crowd grew suddenly quiet. The silence got through to Jamie. He seemed to become terribly aware of the crowd. He froze.

Jack dribbled the ball past Jamie. "Hey," he said, "let's set up Stringer with his tip-in shot."

Jamie's trance was broken.

They moved into the play.

Stringer was in the right position at the right second. Sure enough, he came through with his tip-in shot.

The score was 22 to 24: Blue Rangers ahead!

The Red Devils—time conscious and behind by two points—rushed the ball down the court. Their center put in a jump shot. The game was tied at 24 to 24.

There were two minutes to go in the overtime.

Now both teams were so edgy that when a foul was called on Jack, the fouled Red Devil forward missed his free throw.

Tension mounted.

Seconds clicked off. Neither team could break through for the winning shot.

Mrs. Miller, up in the stands, said, "I just can't watch. I'm going to turn my back."

"Just don't start hiccuping," said her husband.

The crowd roared. She turned and looked at the scoreboard. The Red Devils had made a basket. The score was 26 to 24.

The clock moved steadily on.

The Red Devils were putting on a stall.

The Blue Rangers were in a close man-to-man defense. Jamie nipped in and snagged the ball. He drove in and went up for the lay-up shot. The ball had just left his fingers when the referee's whistle and the timer's horn blew at the same time. The clock stood at zero.

The ball lazed around the rim. Every eye was glued on it. If it didn't go in, it was the Red Devils' game.

Quietly the ball settled within the rim and swished through the basket. 28 to 28!

The crowd roared.

The referee held up his hands to calm the crowd—and to get his message across. A Red Devil had fouled Jamie while he was shooting the basket.

One free throw was awarded to Jamie. This would be the telling shot for the championship, and Jamie knew it. As he came to the free throw line, he started to hiccup.

"This goes on your chart," whispered Jack.

Jamie tossed the ball.

It dropped through the net.

The Blue Rangers had won. By one point. The scoreboard read:

Red Devils: 28

Blue Rangers: 29

6 • Who's the Hero?

Jack knew Jamie had never had his hand shaken so much. Or had his back slapped so much. Or been hugged so much.

And, Jack thought, looking over at his twin, Jamie'd never smiled so much.

Maybe Jamie would decide that this was what basketball was all about. Team playing. Not just shooting baskets by yourself, but playing with a team. Making mistakes wasn't all that bad. It was part of the game. Everyone goofed some time.

First the team all congratulated each other. Then they were all congratulated by everyone else. They telephoned Fred and Andy to tell them the good news. They recapped the game with the coach. Then they congratulated each other again.

When the twins finally went outside, Mr. and Mrs. Miller and Jill were waiting for them at the car, all smiles.

"Okay, fellows, off for a celebration treat," said Mr. Miller.

"Gee, guys, you were great," Jill said. "Emily nearly fainted, she was so excited, Jack. And Nancy thinks Jamie is fantastic. She's writing you a note tonight, Jamie."

"I'm absolutely limp," said Mrs. Miller. "I couldn't do this every day! And I was only watching!"

"Talk about being hungry!" said Jamie, as the Miller family arrived at the pizza parlor to celebrate the victory. "I could eat my weight in pizzas. A basketball game is a lot of work!"

They all piled out of the car and went into

the brightly lighted, cheerful neighborhood restaurant.

Al Tenuta looked up from behind the counter where he was ringing up a bill on the cash register. "Bet you're all celebrating, huh?" he asked, smiling. "Guess the Miller family really has something to celebrate tonight. The news is all over town."

"We're really celebrating, all right," said Mr. Miller. "Cheese and mushroom pizzas all around for this crew."

They sat down around one of the tables.

"News must travel fast," said Mrs. Miller. "The game's been over for only half an hour."

At another table, someone familiar smiled and waved. He called: "Congratulations!"

They smiled back. "Who's that?" asked Jill.

"A neighbor down the block," said Mrs. Miller. "I forget his name."

"It makes me feel silly, having everyone think we're heroes or something," said Jack.

As they ate their pizzas, other neighbors came in, smiled, and waved greetings. "To think we live on the same street!" called one.

The boys waved back. "Thanks," said Jamie.

"How does everybody know about our winning the game?" Jack asked.

"Good news travels fast, I guess," said Mrs. Miller. She looked over at Jill, who seemed to be talking to herself.

"What are you saying?" she asked. "Speak up, dear."

"Listen to this one," said Jill. "It's a cheer I just made up:

> The bases are loaded—
> Can't stand the suspense.
> Hit it! Hit it!
> Over the fence."

Jill swung at an imaginary ball and nearly knocked over her water glass.

"What on earth is that about?" asked Mrs. Miller.

"Wait! Don't tell me," said Jack. "You're

thinking about baseball season!"

"Well, basketball season's over now, isn't it?" asked Jill. "This was the last game."

"That's what I call thinking ahead," laughed Jamie.

Al Tenuta came over to their table, grinning broadly.

"How's it feel to be famous?" he asked.

"I guess we didn't realize everyone was so interested in Boys Club basketball," said Mr. Miller. "It's very nice, very rewarding, to see this reaction."

"Basketball?" asked Al, puzzled. "You play basketball?"

Mr. Miller looked around the table. They all looked at Al Tenuta.

"Well—I thought—that is, well . . . what ARE we celebrating, Al? Perhaps *you'd* better tell *us.*"

"You don't know what you're celebrating?" asked Al. "Well—better to show than to tell. Wait—I'll get it."

He went over to the counter and reached under it. In a moment he was back with the newspaper.

"Read all about it," he said cheerfully, handing the paper to Mr. Miller. "Front page hero."

Al went back to the cash register to check out a customer.

The boys and Jill jumped up to look over their father's shoulder as he looked at the paper.

There on the front page was a picture of Baron. *Their* Baron.

"Baron!" exclaimed Jamie. "It can't be—but it is!"

Mr. Miller read the caption under the picture aloud: "DOG TURNS HIMSELF IN."

"Hurry up," said Mrs. Miller. "I can't stand any more suspense today."

Mr. Miller glanced at the news story briefly, grinned, and started reading.

"Knowing the new city ordinances against dogs that are roaming the streets, Baron, the dog of Mr. and Mrs. John Miller and family, of 568 Mapleton Street, yesterday decided to give himself up. He chased the dogcatcher's truck all the way to the city pound, where he is already well known. He made himself at home while he awaited the arrival of his owner. When asked why he did it, Baron wagged his tail, as if to say, 'No comment.'"

There was silence for a moment as the children sat down again.

"Baron," said Jamie. "Dad, let me read what it says about that dog again."

"Good for him," said Jack. "Front page stuff. And we thought *we* were the heroes," he added. "We thought everyone was cheering *us.*"

"Well, they were, dear, at the game," said Mrs. Miller. "After all, the Blue Rangers did beat the Red Devils."

"Baron wins! If you can't lick 'em, join 'em," said Mr. Miller. "Think we can find a special bone?"

"He's probably already eaten your Christmas slippers by now, Dad," said Jamie jokingly. "I bet he's really had a wonderful time with them while we've been gone and he's had the house to himself."

Mr. Miller groaned. "I feel in my bones that you're right," he said. "Let's get home and rescue what's left of my slippers—and of the house!"

"I know what I'm going to do as soon as

we're back," said Jill. "I'm going to do a cheer for Baron!"

By the time the car pulled into the driveway, Jack, Jamie, and Jill were chanting:

"Baron, Baron,
On the beam,
Come on, Baron,
Join our team!"